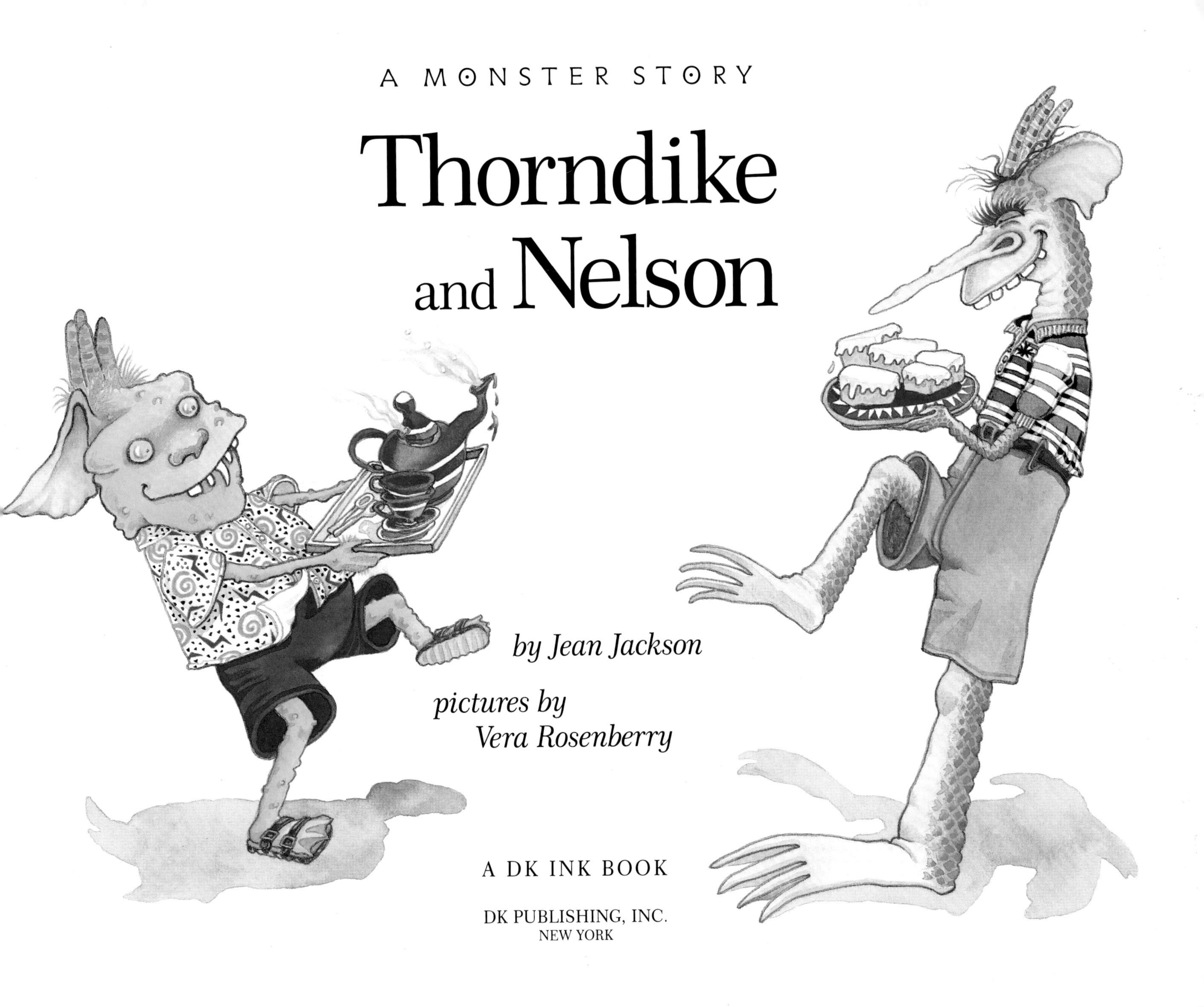

A MONSTER STORY

Thorndike and Nelson

by Jean Jackson

pictures by Vera Rosenberry

A DK INK BOOK

DK PUBLISHING, INC.
NEW YORK

To the memory of Alice M. Bregman—J.J.

To Venki, my co-monster and best friend—V.R.

A DK INK BOOK
2 4 6 8 10 9 7 5 3 1
DK Publishing, Inc., 95 Madison Avenue, New York, NY 10016
Visit us on the World Wide Web at http://www.dk.com

Manufactured in the United States of America. Printed by Barton Press, Inc.
Bound by Horowitz/Rae.
The text of this book is set in 16 pt. Primer.
The illustrations are ink and watercolor paintings reproduced in full color.
Library of Congress cataloging is available upon request.
ISBN 0-7894-2452-5

Every morning two monsters met under a poison apple tree to sip bubbling swamp water from small blue teacups and nibble sweet sticky treats with lemon frosting. Their names were Thorndike and Nelson.

And every morning Nelson's dog, Dot, prowled the neighborhood until she found an unattended item of footwear, which she speared with one long white fang and brought back to her master.

"Look what Dot found this time," Nelson said. "A big pink slipper!"

Thorndike jumped up so fast his stump fell over backwards. "That's *my* slipper!" he cried. "That…that…that smelly mutt stole my slipper. And it was brand-new, too!"

“What did you call Dot?” Nelson asked, puffing up with anger.

“I called her a smelly mutt!” Thorndike said. “Only a smelly mutt would steal a slipper and chew a hole in it.”

“Nobody calls Dot a smelly mutt and gets away with it,” Nelson said. He picked up the pot of bubbling swamp water and poured it over his best friend’s head.

“Yeeoooowwww!” Thorndike screeched.

"You are going to be very sorry you did that!" Thorndike shouted. "Very, very sorry." Then he turned and ran through the thistles and weeds and swamp grass to Nelson's house.

"Stop!" Nelson yelled, running after him. "Come back! What are you going to do?"

Dot looked up with mild interest. Then — gulp — she swallowed the big pink slipper.

Thorndike grabbed Nelson's cookie jar and emptied all of his chocolate-covered lizards down the kitchen sink. Nelson gasped.

Chocolate-covered lizards were his favorite snack. He covered his eyes with his big hairy hands and cried.

Nelson blew his nose and wiped his eyes. Then he ran across the street to Thorndike's house.

"Don't you dare!" Thorndike yelled. "Nelson, I'm warning you!"

Nelson darted through Thorndike's front door and up the stairs to his bedroom. He grabbed Thorndike's bat wings and emptied the box out the window.

“Not my bat wing collection,” Thorndike wailed as he watched the tissue-thin wings flutter slowly to the ground.

Thorndike ran back to Nelson's house. He pulled the garage door open and let the air out of all seven tires on Nelson's sharkmobile.

Spinning around so fast he tripped and almost fell, Nelson raced back to Thorndike's house.

“Stay off my property!” Thorndike yelled. “No trespassing!”

Nelson ran to the bookcase where Thorndike kept his jar of pet spiders. He unscrewed the lid and set them free — all 1,128 of them.

Thorndike fell to the floor. “My spiders!” he cried. “They’re getting away! Come back, Sam! Come back, Tina! Boris and Fred and Mona and Lisa — come back!”

But none of the spiders came back.

“Nelson, you have done it this time,” Thorndike said. “This time you have really done it.”

Thorndike made a beeline for Nelson's prize-winning skunk cabbage patch.

"Nooooooooo!" Nelson howled in horror. "Not my prize-winning skunk cabbage patch!"

Thorndike was reaching for Nelson's biggest, most stinky blossom when he heard a noise under the juniper tree. It was Dot.

"Call the police!" Nelson yelled.
"Call the fire department!
Call the President of the United States!
Dot is choking!"

Nelson grabbed Dot by her feet
and shook her upside down.

When that didn’t work, he slapped her on the back. Dot made a small gasping noise, then collapsed.

"Don't die, Dot!" Nelson sobbed. Big salty tears sprayed from his eyes. "Please don't die!"

"Step back," Thorndike said, finally pushing Nelson aside. He wrapped his arms around Dot's middle, clasped his hands under her rib cage, and squeezed up.

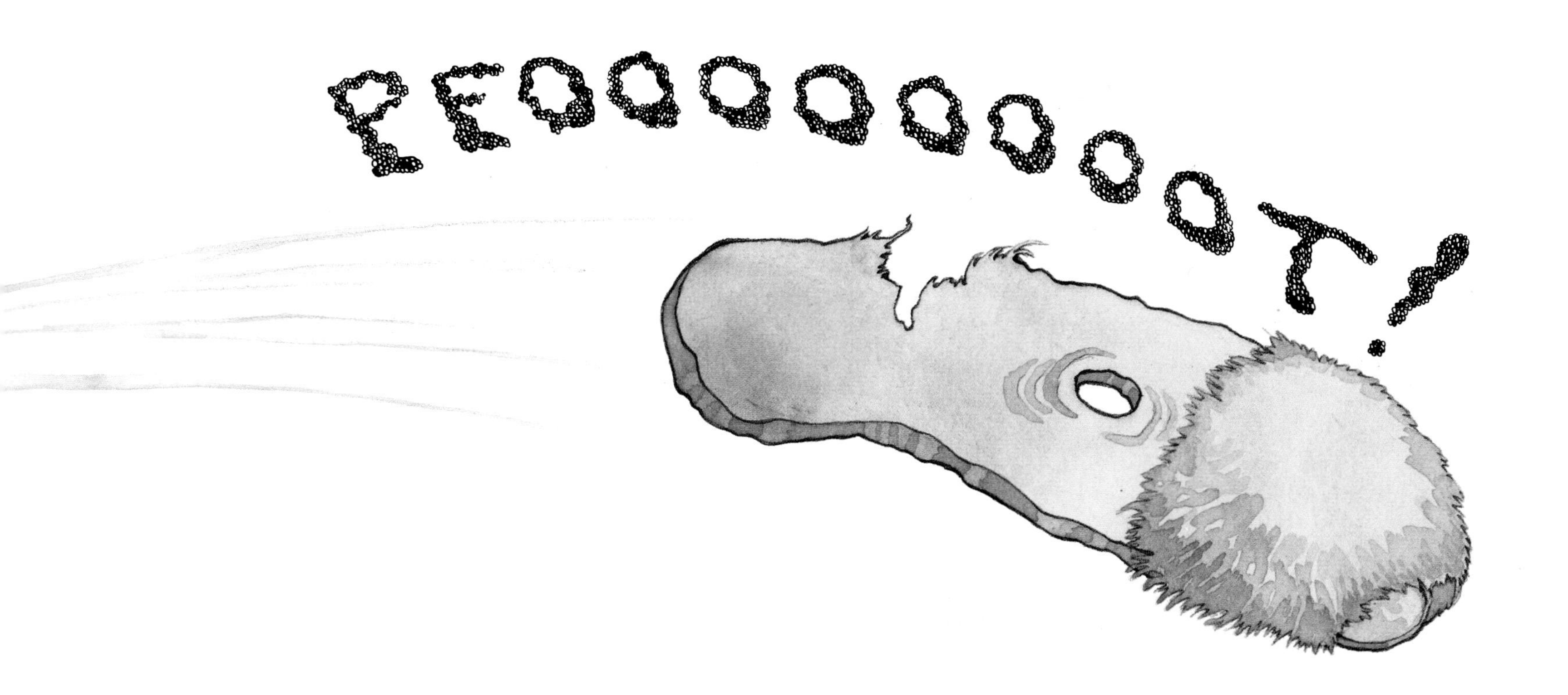

Out popped the big pink slipper.

“You saved Dot’s life!” Nelson cried, giving Thorndike a big bear hug. “Thank you, thank you, thank you!”

Dot jumped up and licked Thorndike’s nose.

"I'm sorry I called Dot a smelly mutt," Thorndike said to Nelson. "My mouth spoke before my brain could stop it."

Nelson slapped his right hand with his left. "That's what you get for pouring bubbling swamp water on Thorndike's head," he said to his hand. "Don't ever do it again!"

Thorndike used a wrench to open the pipe under Nelson's sink and retrieve his chocolate-covered lizards.

Very carefully, Nelson picked up Thorndike's bat wings.

Thorndike pumped the air back into the sharkmobile's tires.

Nelson gathered up Thorndike's pet spiders — all 1,128 of them.

"I'm glad we're friends again," Nelson said as he dropped the last spider back into the jar on Thorndike's bookcase.

"Me, too," Thorndike replied. "Fighting gives me indigestion."

"It makes my stomach hurt," Nelson said.

Then, arm in arm, the two monsters headed for Thorndike's house,

where they made a fresh pot of bubbling swamp water and a big platter of frosted lemon bars to eat under the poison apple tree.

As for Dot, she never picked up another shoe, sock, slipper, or boot. She did, however, begin to bring home assorted undergarments…